I
don't like
it!

For Klaus and Audrey

With grateful thanks to Anne Wilkinson, designer of the doll

I don't like it!

Ruth Brown

RED FOX

A Red Fox Book
Published by Arrow Books Limited
20 Vauxhall Bridge Road, London SW1V 2SA

An imprint of the Random Century Group
London, Melbourne, Sydney, Auckland
Johannesburg and agencies throughout the world

First published by Andersen Press Ltd. 1989

Red Fox edition 1990

Made and printed in Italy by Grafiche AZ, Verona

ISBN 0 09 970240 1

The little doll sighed – "I'm sad!" she cried.
"I knew things would change. I don't like it!
It's not the same since that puppy came
And it's such a shame. I don't like it!

"She loves him more than me, I'm sure
They play all the time and I hate it!
But if I want to play, then they just go away –
So why shouldn't I say: I don't like it!

"Perhaps it's just me. Hey, toys! Can you see
How everything's changed. Do you like it?"
Ted lay on his bed and raising his head
He sleepily said: "I don't mind it!

"It means I can rest which is what I do best
'Cos I'm lazy and fat and I like it.
I snooze and I dream that I'm eating ice-cream
With the honey-bee queen. Yes! I love it!"

"I might have known you wouldn't moan.
I'll ask Jack-in-the-Box if he likes it.
Hey, you over there! I've just asked the bear
If he thinks it's fair. Do you mind it?"

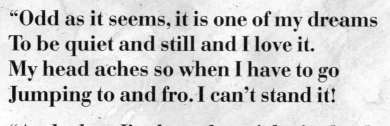

"Odd as it seems, it is one of my dreams
To be quiet and still and I love it.
My head aches so when I have to go
Jumping to and fro. I can't stand it!

"And when I'm boxed up tight, in the dark dark night,
I quake and I shake and I hate it!
But when I'm out and I'm lying about
There's no shadow of a doubt — that I like it!"

"Well the mice aren't like you – they want something to do!
I'll call them and see if they mind it."
So she knelt on the floor to knock on their door
And asked like before: "Do you like it?"

A tiny grey mouse stepped out of the house
And said: "Yes, we really enjoy it!
We've never had time to clean up the grime
And to polish and shine — and we love it!"

"Listen to you! You're too good to be true!
If they'd got a cat, would you like it?"
But the mouse turned around and with hardly a sound
Started sweeping the ground. She did like it!

"I'm the only one who wants any fun!"
The little doll sighed – but she wasn't –

For when later on everybody had gone
And the house was totally silent…

Someone else came that way, also wanting to play
Saw the doll where it lay – and he liked it!

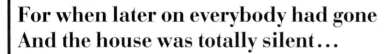

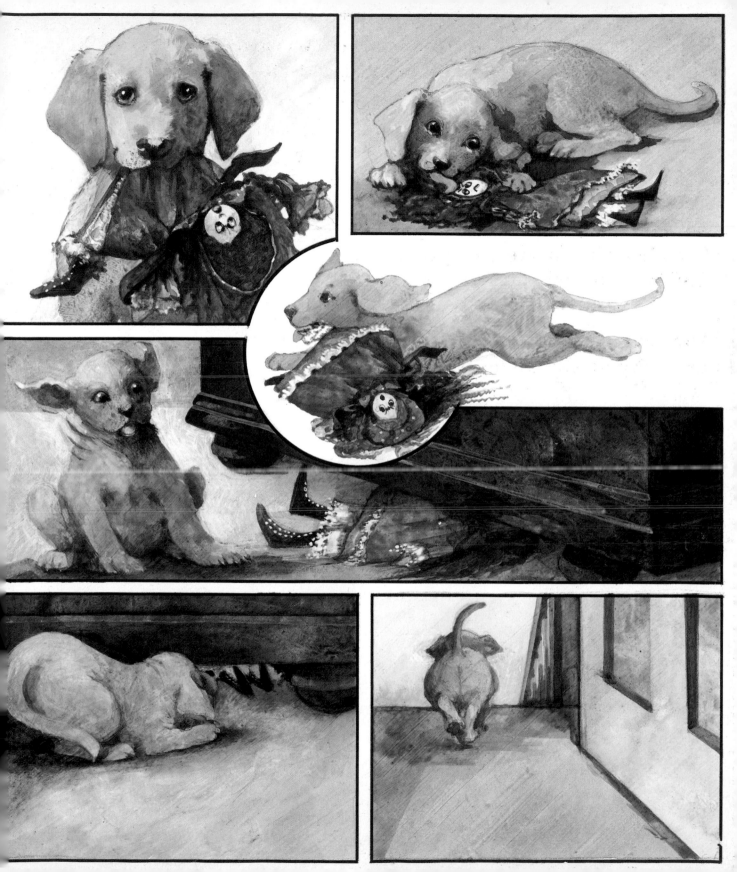

That night Mum said: "It's time for bed.
Where's your doll gone? Can you see it?"
So they searched everywhere – on the floor, on the stair –
But it just wasn't there! "We can't find it!

"It's lost, you see – where can it be?"
The little girl sobbed. "I want it!"
"Don't cry so, dear – it must be near.
Look! Puppy's here! Go fetch it!

"He's done it too! It's as if he knew
That your doll was there – and he found it!
Well, I'll say goodnight and switch off the light.
Will you be all right, now you've got it?"

But there came no reply, not a stir, not a sigh,
For the girl was asleep now she'd found it.
And the little doll smiled, snuggled close to the child,
With a cry soft and mild: "That's more like it!"

Other titles in the Red Fox picture book series (also incorporating Beaver Books)

Not Like That, Like This Tony Bradman & Debbie Van Der Beek
If At First You Do Not See Ruth Brown
I Don't Like It Ruth Brown
The Cross With Us Rhinocerous John Bush & Paul Geraghty
The Proud and Fearless Lion Reg Cartwright
Ellie's Doorstep Alison Catley
Who's Ill Today? Lynne Cherry
Herbie the Dancing Hippo Charlotte Van Emst
The Angel and the Wild Animal Michael Foreman
Joe Eats Bugs Susanne Gretz
Old Bear Jane Hissey
Little Bear's Trousers Jane Hissey
Bad Boris and the birthday Susie Jenkin Pearce
My Grandma Has Black Hair Mary Hoffman and Joanna Burroughs
Best Friends Stephen Kellog
Jake Deborah King
When Sheep Cannot Sleep Satoshi Kitamura
Coco's Birthday Surprise Agnes Matthieu & Angela Sommer-Bodenburg
The Stiltons: Albert and Albertine Moira & Colin Maclean
Not Now, Bernard David McKee
The Sad Story of Veronica who played the Violin David McKee
Snow Woman David McKee
Who's a Clever Baby Then? David McKee
Stories for Summer Alf Prøysen
Mrs Pepperpot and the Macaroni Alf Prøysen
Bad Mood Bear John Richardson
Stone Soup Tony Ross
The Three Pigs Tony Ross
Oscar Got the Blame Tony Ross
A Witch got on at Paddington Station Dyan Sheldon & Wendy Smith
If I were a Crocodile Rowena Sommerville
The Monster Bed Susan Varley & Jeanne Willis
Mucky Mabel Jeanne Willis & Margaret Chamberlain
The Tale of Georgie Grub Jeanne Willis & Margaret Chamberlain
Maggie and the Monster Elizabeth Winthrop & Tomie de Paola